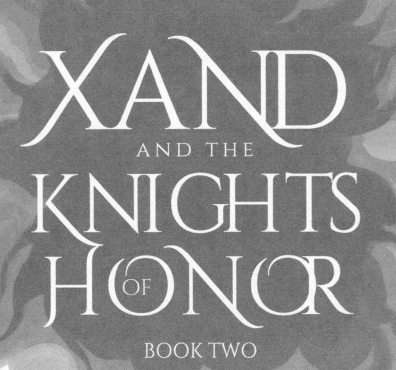

XAND AND THE KNIGHTS OF HONOR

BOOK TWO

The Battle of the Giant

JAX WARD

THE BATTLE OF THE GIANT
BOOK TWO OF THE KNIGHTS OF HONOR SERIES

© 2021 Jax Ward

Print ISBN: 978-1-66781-2-557

CONTENTS

PROLOGUE

The space station gently floated through an empty dark abyss as meteors and debris zoomed around it. The moon outside the large window of the main observation room reflected the closest star, bathing the room and the imposing figure within it in a pale light.

"The Gargoyle King must bring me what he has promised," the deep voice rumbled, "or he will see his last." A nearby crewmember, uncertain of whether the figure was talking to him, stumbled into his words. "Uh, yes, yes, my Lord, we will make, uh, sure that he keeps his end of the deal." The figure nodded slightly and turned away.

"Good." The grim response hung in the silent, artificial air, harmonizing with the slow, dull tone of the buzzing machines keeping the station afloat.

CHAPTER

ONE

"It has to be us!" Xand pleaded to Jork. "Don't you see? Whatever happened a few days ago was magical and important."

Jork shook his head. "You have no idea what happened or why it did. You are just a boy! Too young to understand! And Zeg, I love him, I do. But Zeg," Jork paused, uncertain of how to describe his son, who stood larger than most men but sometimes acted like a child half his age. "Zeg sometimes isn't good at staying on task," he finally allowed, unable to say anything more at all about his son.

"Look, Zeg needs to come with us. I know we are young. But that Shield, and Sparkie, I don't know why or what it is, but it feels like we are *supposed* to go, that is supposed to be us." Xand looked down and chose his following words carefully. "I know you fought in the Great War, and I know you did everything you could, but –"

Jork stood up and cut Xand off, as angry as Xand had ever seen him. "You know nothing about the Great War! Zeg is only a child. I cannot risk his life just to destroy some gargoyles!"

"Some Gargoyles? Those gargoyles are going to kill thousands of millions of people," Xand said. "We have to do something."

Xand was surprised by Jork's reaction. Their lives had all drastically changed just a few days ago when the Gargoyle King's army had attacked Xand's hometown of Zendora.

After the dramatic rescue efforts by Xand and his newly assembled group of friends, a celebration had taken place. But after the festival, the reality of their new situation took hold. For Xand, the experience brought a mix of emotions. He was happy he could defend his people, yet afraid because he felt like he had been chosen to fight the Gargoyle King, a much bigger responsibility than he thought he would ever have. Xand was confused about how his Shield had seemingly come to life to help him win the battle.

Wilder and Yama, Xand's old and newest friends, had spoken with him about the Shield and what it meant. Neither could agree on the source of its magic or why it worked for Xand the way it did, but Wilder knew it had been an essential part of the Great War against the Gargoyle King, and therefore it was important that Xand was able to wield it.

With all those things in mind, Xand had gone to sleep the night before his current argument with Jork and slept restlessly. The next day he felt as if a pack of wild horses had run over him. His dreams had been strange, and he remembered only bits and pieces. In one, he was battling in a kingdom with large castles made of metal, iron chariots moving without horses, strange-looking creatures holding metal that shot fire. In the dream, as an explosion shook the sky, his friends on either side of him disappeared, popping out of existence, until finally, he himself disappeared. In another, he fought the Gargoyle King in person, hand-to-hand. While Xand grew weary, the Gargoyle King seemed to get stronger and stronger until finally, a huge punch landed on Xand's head, and he woke screaming and covering his face from the imagined terrible fist.

Tired after this nightmare-filled night, Xand gathered his most prized belongings he thought he might need for his journey. His newly found Shield, his sword, some food, a small blue stone that his parents had given him when he was a baby before they were taken away by goblins on the worst day of his life, an ink-stained map, and all of the money he had saved up over the years working on his grandparent's farm and selling small items at the market.

After gathering what he needed, he went to Jork's to talk about Zeg. It had not gone as he had planned.

Xand knew that Jork was simply scared of losing Zeg. Jork never talked about the Great War, but Xand knew there must have been something terrible that he saw that made him so afraid now.

"I know you wanted him to be a blacksmith," said Xand.

Jork shook his head as he cleaned his hands on his apron. "Zeg does not love the idea of blacksmithing, and he has been talking non-stop about your last adventure," said Jork. "But you don't understand what you are getting into. If you leave Zendora to go off and search for glory and battles, all you will find is suffering and death."

Xand had never seen Jork so serious before.

"I don't know what to say. Zeg is my best friend, and I would never do anything to put him in harms' way. What we are about to do is dangerous," said Xand, his head bowed. "But I need him with me."

"I know that," Jork whispered. "Zeg thinks this is a game, and I do not want him to think otherwise," said Jork. "We did everything we could to defeat the Gargoyle King in my day. It took everything we had – adults, mind you – to defeat him. And we didn't even succeed! You don't understand how hard that was. What is your plan? How are you going to do it?"

"I will take care of Zeg, I promise," said Xand. "And I know you did everything you could, but it wasn't enough. Maybe the Shield chose us because we don't have a plan. And maybe doing it different than you did will work." Xand grew excited as he spoke and then paused, considering how young and immature he sounded. "I don't know. But I know that if we don't do it, no one else will. And if we can't do it, maybe no one can."

Jork stared up at the ceiling of his shop, looking at the sharp metal objects he had forged over the years, with tears beginning to form in his eyes. Then he nodded and moved back towards the anvil where he had been working when Xand burst into his shop that morning.

"Go wake him up. He is still asleep," he said in a hushed whisper.

CHAPTER

TWO

"**W**ell, Zeg, you seem to be very excited about this adventure," said Wilder. They had been on the road for half the day. For most of the journey, Zeg kept talking about every small detail he could remember of the fight: the smell of the ground, the color of the force field, how one of the guards had passed out in horror at the incoming zombies. He brought everything up the second it came to his mind.

For Wilder, this was something he would expect from such a young dwarf, especially since he had never been outside of the town area or had seen much action. For Yama, it was intriguing and exciting to learn as many details as possible to satisfy her thirst for knowledge of the world outside the Tree.

Xand tried not to mind Zeg. Wilder had spoken to Xand at first to warn him this would continue for days on end, and it would repeat itself as soon as they achieved another victory and the next one after that. Xand smiled back and nodded with Wilder when the werewolf explained all of this to him, but Xand could not ignore his concerns about Zeg.

"It will be great. We will fight again and beat the Gargoyle King!" exclaimed Zeg excitedly. "He does not know what is coming towards him!" Zeg punched the air with both hands, almost hitting Wilder in the process, who simply sighed with resignation.

"Slow down, Zeg," said Wilder. "First, we need to get supplies from the next village, and then we can decide where our next great adventure will be ok?"

Wilder had explained to the group that it would be best to acquire the tools they needed outside of Zendora to avoid others trying to join them in their dangerous quest. Keeping Zeg safe would be hard enough, thought Wilder. He knew that Yama could handle herself, at least during the day. As for Xand, while usually Wilder would have to keep both Xand and Zeg safe, he realized the Shield changed this.

As they approached the village, Yama's excitement grew. "Xand, I wanted to ask you," she said. "Would you mind if we took some time in the village to meet with some of the people?"

"It's ok, but we need to remember what we're doing here, which is to get supplies so we can stop the Gargoyle King. Let's not get too distracted," replied Xand. Xand did not want to risk finding the army or other minions of the Gargoyle King during the night like they did last time.

"Thank you, thank you!" said Yama, her voice full of excitement at the prospect. She turned back to Zeg, who was as excited as she was. "You heard that, Zeg. We will have time to meet some people in the village!"

"I can tell them all about our latest victory!" said Zeg, who started clapping and jumping with joy while Wilder just rolled his eyes at Xand.

"Well, this is going to be a fine adventure, right, Sparkie?" asked Wilder as he looked at Sparkie. The horse simply ignored the remark and continued on his way while Xand shook his head in disbelief at how the situation was developing.

CHAPTER

THREE

"There it is—Naran," said Wilder. The group had stopped at an intersection that would take them to places only Wilder knew about. To the north, they could see a small village in the distance with fields on all sides of it.

"Looks smaller than Zendora," said Zeg. He covered his eyes to shield himself from the sun's rays and looked closer. "Much smaller."

"There is not much in Naran. The good thing about it is finding bedding, food, and some of the supplies we will need to continue. Not much more than that, to be honest," said Wilder. He scratched his forehead as he examined the surrounding area. "And nothing much has changed around here, either."

"How often do you come here?" asked Xand. Wilder laughed at the question.

"Xand, I come here every month and have done so for some years now. Believe me, this place is the same as usual, and not that interesting. If we are in luck, we may find Madam Lauren to serve us some of her stew," said Wilder. Zeg and Yama looked impressed at what Wilder had just said. They had never tasted Madam Lauren's stew and could not wait to try.

"You know everyone here, huh?" Yama asked him. Wilder nodded.

"Yes, I know them and have spoken with all of them at one point or another. Come, the sun is killing me right now," said Wilder, giving a sidelong glance at Yama. As they walked into the village, a small group of townspeople greeted Wilder with surprise and remarked at how soon he had returned after his last visit.

Yama was surprised at how the humans had rapidly greeted Wilder and how excited they were to talk to him; she had thought little about him, but seeing how they behaved, she thought he could not be as bad as she had originally imagined. While Yama had only just met Wilder, the fact that her magic came from the sun and his the moon meant she had an instant natural distrust for him. And it appeared the feeling was mutual.

Zeg tried to tell the group about his recent adventures, but they did not seem to understand his wild statements or why he was waiving his arms around and would not listen to him. They were more interested in talking to Wilder about how everything was going at Zendora and the surrounding villages.

Xand was worried that they would draw too much attention to themselves, but seeing that they were more interested in Wilder and talking about what was going on in the world, he sighed with relief and started looking around for a place to let Sparkie rest and eat.

"Now, let me present you to some of my friends here. We are traveling far away for a one-time trip to a very remote location. When we come back, we can talk all about it," said Wilder. He presented Xand, Sparkie, Yama, and Zeg to the villagers, who greeted them as excitedly as they had initially welcomed Wilder.

When Wilder finished his introductions, they went back to talking with him. Still, he politely explained that he was needed to help his friends prepare to continue their adventure.

"I know, I know, we can talk more later today, but for now, we would like to rest and have some time to talk about what needs to be done. If there is stew later, I will be sure to be there for everyone," said Wilder to the older woman standing close to him, who nodded and clapped in excitement while the rest agreed.

"I will have extra for everyone, although it will be heavy on the vegetibles this time because of…" she paused and trailed off. "Anyway, how grateful I am to have you back here with us!" said Madam Lauren. The villagers allowed the group to continue walking as they all dispersed back to where they had been, with an extra pep in their step from the exciting events of the morning.

"They rarely get to meet someone from the outside," explained Wilder. "I have come here for so many years that I have become the village pet of sorts. I do not like the term, but I understand their intentions." He smirked and scratched the back of his neck. "Say, you don't really mind if we take a rest, right?"

"I think Sparkie could use some water and would enjoy some time resting as well," said Xand. He looked at the rest of the group.

"I'll talk about our adventures while we rest!" said Zeg. Wilder rolled his eyes.

As they were moving towards the well at the center of the village, a young boy sat beside it while drinking from the bucket next to it. A brown dog sitting near him also drank from the bucket when the boy put it down.

"Jack, it has been a long time since I last saw you," said Wilder. "You weren't around the last time I was here."

Jack looked up to see Wilder coming over to him and stood up immediately. "Wilder, it has been a long time!" said Jack. "How have you been?"

"Life is good, life is good. Say, when did you get a fellow canine?" asked Wilder. Jack looked back at the dog and then at Wilder.

"This? Oh, I got it a while ago, but he's not much use. This dog is just lazy and couldn't care less about life," said Jack. Wilder arched both eyebrows at the statement.

"How so? Looks like he is fine," said Wilder. Jack patted his left leg to clear off some dust and pointed at the dog.

"He looks fine, but he doesn't like to do anything. I have tried to get him to help me, to train him. Nothing. He just likes to sit around," said Jack. Wilder nodded and approached the dog, who began moving his tail around wildly. "That's the first time I have seen him do that," the boy said.

"*What is your name?*" asked Wilder in werewolf language. The strange growls and sounds he produced confused Jack. Xand and Zeg had seen him do it a few times and had never gotten used to it, while Yama was disgusted and horrified.

"*You can speak to me?*" asked the dog, through barks that only Wilder could understand.

"*I am just like you, in a way. My name is Wilder. What is yours?*" asked Wilder, with a set of growls, howls, and barks more complex and stranger than before.

"*I am Jenni. Pleased to meet you, Wilder,*" answered Jenni.

"*What are you doing here?*" asked Wilder. The dog stood to walk on four legs and pointed at a distant range of mountains with his nose.

"*I came from the mountains. I got lost. This human found me but insists that I do his work for him,*" answered Jenni. Wilder nodded at what Jenni told him while the others moved their heads back and forth between the two creatures taking turns barking at each other.

"*For food, you work. That is always a thing with humans. What do you want me to tell him for you?*" asked Wilder. Jenni sat back and cocked his head to the side while thinking.

"*That I only wish to sit by this well and have some water and food. I like to look at things around me, not work. I don't like working and I am too old for that,*" answered Jenni. "*And that my name is Jenni, and he should respect my choices.*" Wilder nodded and looked back at Jack.

"That was an interesting conversation," said Wilder. Jack looked very confused and surprised at Wilder, then at Jenni.

"You can talk to dogs?" asked Jack. Wilder nodded and raised his left hand with an open palm.

"To canines. 'Dogs' is too… simple," said Wilder, who continued. "Jenni here wants me to tell you something."

"Jenni? That's his name? How does a dog… a canine, have a name if I haven't given him one?" asked Jack. Wilder sighed and put his right hand over Jack's left shoulder.

"Humans don't give names to canines. You think you do, but everyone has a name. His name is Jenni, and he has an important message for you," said Wilder. Jack looked terrified as Wilder got closer to him. "He likes to sit, have some water and food, and see things around him as they are happening, to just enjoy life. He's earned that in his old age."

"What? ... I mean, I just can't feed him if he is going to sit around all day and—," said Jack. Wilder stepped even closer to the boy, so close the boy could smell Wilder's breath, and it reminded him of what Jenni's smelled like. "Fine, fine, I will make sure Jenni has a good life and doesn't have to work."

"Thank you," said Wilder, slowly backing away from Jack.

"I will make sure he has a good life and doesn't have to work, if," Jack said, letting the "if" hang and float around for a beat before continuing. "If, you can help us with something, please," said Jack, who lowered his voice as he tried approaching Wilder again. "We can't talk very loud about this; people are too scared."

"I shouldn't have to bargain for something you should be doing anyway. But if the people in this town are scared of something, I will help," said Wilder. "Tell us everything."

CHAPTER

FOUR

J ack nodded but asked Wilder and the rest of
the group to follow him to a nearby cobble-
stone and wood house where he lived. Once inside,
Jack made sure the door was closed and secured
so no one would suddenly drop into the middle of
their conversation.

As the group moved into the house, Xand made
sure to tie Sparkie next to the well. He saw how Zeg
had trouble getting into the house and had to kneel
down on the ground to fit into the place properly
without bursting through the thatch roof.

"Wilder, have you heard about the Giant?"
asked Jack. The group looked surprised at
Wilder, who looked back at them and then shook
his head.

"No, I have not heard anything about a Giant. What are you talking about?" asked Wilder. Jack sighed as he sat down on a small stool.

"It all began about two days after the last time you were here. A Giant came into the fields and started eating the livestock… it has been horrible ever since then," said Jack. Now Wilder realized why something seemed amiss when he was examining the village from the crossroads.

"That's why there are no animals in the grassland. Did the Giant get everything?" asked Wilder. Jack shrugged and shook his head.

"I don't know. I don't think so, but the giant is very smart and has been figuring out ways to get them no matter what we do. Wilder, we really need your help. This is not just for me. It's for everyone," said Jack. Wilder sighed as he heard this and looked back at the group.

"I guess this is the next part of our adventure," said Wilder. Zeg and Yama were excited at the thought, while Xand looked worried at having to face a Giant.

"That Giant doesn't sound like a problem. I can lift a cow, so it will be a fair fight," said Zeg, who stretched his arms and showed his muscles.

"I am pretty sure the Giant is far bigger than you, much bigger in fact," said Jack. He looked at the roof of the house and bobbed his head, saying, "Much, much bigger than you."

"I can imagine," said Wilder. He looked at Xand, who then looked back at him straight in the eyes. "What do you think?" he wanted to know.

"It's dangerous… but it may be related to . . . , you know," said Xand. Wilder agreed by slowly nodding his head.

"The Gargoyle King stands no chance against us!" said Zeg. He punched the air and broke part of the roof with his right fist. "I'm sorry," he said. "I'll fix that for you."

CHAPTER

FIVE

The group had traveled to the nearby grass-lands where Jack said the villagers had last seen the Giant. They had a hard time moving through the long grass but had found some proof that the creature had been around the area from its large footprints.

"How big do you think the Giant is?" asked Yama. She had never seen footprints as big as the ones in front of her, and until recently, she had never seen a creature as tall as Zeg either.

"Pretty big, judging from the footprints. At least three times as tall as Zeg," said Wilder. He had kneeled in the grass to get a closer look. "These are at least a day old. I'm worried, though."

"Why, what's wrong?" asked Xand. He examined the footprints as Wilder had done but realized he did not know what he was looking at or what it meant.

"If the animals have all been eaten or if the villagers are hiding the livestock, there will come a time when the Giant will attack the village. And they will not be able to defend themselves," said Wilder.

Xand continued the line of thought. "And then *they* are the ones that will be eaten," said Xand. Wilder stood up and examined the path created in the grassland.

"The footprints go all the way over to that hill. That thing is probably hiding in a nearby cave or somewhere where it can keep itself safe while sleeping," said Wilder. He examined the surrounding area and the back of the hill not far from them. "If we are in luck, it may be asleep."

"Fighting a sleeping Giant is not something worthy of our adventure," said Zeg. Wilder shook his head at this remark.

"Fighting a Giant is far too dangerous. I know, unfortunately. I have fought a Giant before, together with my sister. I was almost crushed by his fist, but my sister pushed me out of the way," Wilder said, his voice going quieter as he spoke. "She was crushed instead." The words barely escaped his mouth, and he turned away to try to hide the tears forming at the corner of his eyes. Xand had never heard Wilder talk about this before.

Wilder quickly walked away through the grassland, following the footprints.

The group was quiet as they continued on their way, shocked and saddened by what they had just learned from their friend. As they exited the grass-land, they found themselves in an area with seven hills scattered towards the horizon. They climbed the shortest one and found that a small valley formed at the center.

That's where they saw the Giant. They were shocked at his size. He was so immense he filled almost all the valley.But Wilder noticed the creature looked as if it had not fed itself properly in weeks. While the Giant had little muscle left on its body, and he was so malnourished that his ribs were visible through his skin, his size was far taller than what Wilder had speculated.

"That's....That's not possible," said Wilder. He remained silent as he saw the creature sleeping. "That's him, and that's the one who killed my sister."

"This is going to be a great adventure!" said Zeg. His voice was so loud that it echoed through the valley and the surrounding area. Wilder raised both arms at Zeg in a futile attempt to stop the sound coming out of his mouth.

"Zeg, this is not the time!" said Wilder said in a hurried hushed tone. From the bottom of the valley, a loud snore and grunt made everyone's hair raise. They watched in horror as the Giant slowly woke up from its slumber and eyed them as its next meal. "Run, run!" Wilder shouted.

"Wilder, wait!" said Xand. He was too late to catch Wilder, who was running as fast as he could without rolling down the hill. Xand prompted Yama and Zeg to follow, too, but they were stuck where they stood, unable to move as they saw the creature rise to its full height. Zeg's smile slowly turned into a shocked face, his mouth wide open and his eyes even wider.

Jack had told them the Giant was at least three times as high as Zeg and Wilder had guessed he would probably be five times or maybe six. They were both wrong. In fact, the Giant slowly waking up and stretching high was almost eight times as tall as Zeg, with huge hands that ripped one of the hills wide open like it was soft cake.

Zeg looked to where Wilder had run away and started to move in that direction., But Zeg fell to the ground, his legs giving out from under him. "This isn't fun. This isn't just a game like it was in the village. That Giant is real, and that Giant killed

Wilder's sister. I can't fight a real fight. I want to go home."

Even kneeling on the ground, Zeg was as tall as Xand. Xand got up to Zeg's face and looked him in the eyes. "Zeg, are you okay?" Zeg didn't respond. "I know it's scary, but we have to do this. It was real before in the village, it wasn't a game then. Do you understand? It's just as real now. You did it before, and you can do it now. If we can't do this, who can?"

Zeg stared blankly at him, "Someone else. Anyone else. Our parents, the grown-ups, the authorities?"

Xand responded, "They tried last time. They didn't defeat the Gargoyle King, and now we're suffering the consequences. We can do it." He paused, hoping his words made a difference to his friend. "We have to," Xand said softly.

Zeg didn't move. Xand had always been able to talk to Zeg about anything, and make him understand it. But not this, not now.

Zeg whispered, "I don't want to die." Xand started to speak, trying to find the right things to say to reassure his friend that they were not about to die. But no words came out.

CHAPTER

SIX

X and heard something loud behind him. He turned to see the Giant starting to move towards them.

Xand turned back to Zeg. "Look, Zeg, it's okay to be afraid. I'm afraid right now. I was afraid in the village. It's not okay to let your fear hold you back."

"But I'm the strong one. I'm supposed to be strong," Zeg said with pain in his voice. "I don't feel strong right now."

Yama pushed Xand aside and took his place, looking up at Zeg and grabbing his hands.

"The Gargoyle King is strong, and he hasn't conquered our world yet. We have fought against him this long because being strong is not enough. Being the strongest doesn't make you the most powerful," Yama said to him softly, holding his hands in hers, her blue eyes staring at him and filling in with tiny yellowish twinkles until they radiated with golden energy.

"If I'm not the strongest of us, then what use am I against that Giant?" Zeg asked with the pain of the words making his voice croak.

"You are not strong enough, Zeg, but you don't have to be," Yama said. "Anybody can be strong, but *together*, we can be legendary."

Zeg blinked twice, and stared at Yama. His body unfolded with a newfound sense of purpose, the fear falling away as his reached his full height. He turned to the Giant with his arms raised high. "Yippee kay-yay, yippee kay-yo!" he yelled and turned and ran full speed towards the Giant.

Xand tried to stop him, but it was too late. He spun around frantically. "Wilder? Wilder, where are you?" He yelled at the top of his lungs, but Wilder was nowhere to be seen.

Xand turned to see where Zeg had run and then reached for his Shield. He did not think it would be of any help against a Giant of that size, but it was all he had.

"Any ideas?" he asked Yama.

"I have one that might work," said Yama. "Make sure to get out of the way. I will blind it!" A golden light flashed as she transformed into her fairy form and flew right at the creature.

"Yama, what are you doing?" asked Xand. She continued flying as fast as she could towards the Giant.

She had just barely managed to avoid one of the Giant's large hands as she tried to climb higher into the sky. The Giant clapped both hands together, trying to catch Yama or, worse, smash her, but just missed. The wave of wind produced by the Giant was so strong that it pushed her off course.

"Yama, here I come," said Zeg still running toward the Giant. Xand looked at how far Yama had been shoved away and then back at the Giant, who had become enraged at their antics. The Giant had pushed himself out of the hills and was figuring out a way down.

Yama was coming back at full speed towards the Giant. Her hands were forming a large yellow orb, which she managed to aim at the Giant. A bright light flashed out of where the orb had been spinning. Xand was knocked off his feet, and when he tried to get up, the entire world was dark. He couldn't see his hands, the Giant, anything. He put his hands to his face, his eyes burning, and yelled for Zeg.

The Giant had become confused by the blinding light and enraged at what had happened. He swung his arms wildly, almost losing his balance, but managed to stand firm at the top of the hill.

By now, Zeg had almost reached the Giant. Yama began building another orb in her hand as the Giant continued trying to hit her without success.

When the Giant removed his hand from his eyes, Yama threw another giant orb towards his face. While not as powerful as the previous one, it hit the Giant right between his eyes, exploding in another large shower of light that blinded him, making him scream in anger.

While this was happening, Zeg closed the gap and slammed into the left leg of the Giant, which was the one that looked to have the weakest footing on the hill. The Giant swung wildly, hammering into Zeg's body and knocking him down the mountain. Xand could hear Zeg's loud grunt of pain but couldn't see where he was or what was going on. He flailed wildly around in a panic, trying to find the Shield.

Then Xand heard a voice in his head. "Xand, calm. Move your hand over a little bit to the left and up about twice your arm's length." Xand was confused, but followed the direction and could feel the warm, hard edge of the Shield in his hands.

The voice said, "Use my magic to create a barrier around your friend. Then aim me where I tell you and command me to cast your spell. You don't have much time. You must do this now."

Xand stood up and faced the Shield towards where he heard the commotion. He didn't know how to create a barrier, and he didn't know what spell he was supposed to cast or how. Xander knewthat he wanted Zeg to be as safe as if he were dressed in full armor, and he wanted the Giant to never be able to hurt his friends now or ever. With his heart full of those feelings, he thrust the Shield out and commanded it to...to protect Zeg and everyone from the Giant.

Yama was creating another ball of energy to throw at the Giant, who had turned on Zeg with his arms raised to deliver a massive blow. Out of the corner of her eye, she saw a blast of red light. When she turned back, Zeg had a bubble around him, and the Giant's fists were slamming down on it. The red energy rippled out as he made contact with the bubble, and the Giant's shocked face watched as his body began to turn to stone.

His open mouth and terrified eyes were the last part of him that went from flesh to white granite. It was only a matter of seconds, but where before the Giant had stood ready to kill Zeg, now a huge

white statue was left in its place, sinking slightly into

the soft grass before finally settling in for a long,

solid rest.

CHAPTER

SEVEN

Xand called out, "Hello, is anyone there. Is everyone okay? I can't see anything."

Yama and Zeg ran over to him, Yama turning back into human form and helping him up. "You were blinded by my sun energy. You can't look directly at such bright lights, or it will do that to you."

"What do I do now?" Xand asked.

Yama was already acting, waiving her hands around and using energy to create a pair of glasses. She placed them on Xand's face.

The world returned.

"Whoa, I can see perfectly. Yama, did you cure me?"

"Sort of. These glasses will help you see better. Because my fairy magic caused you to go blind, fairy magic can help you see."

Zeg said, "How did you do that? What was that magic."

"I don't know. I heard a voice tell me what to do. And it seemed like it was the Shield, talking about itself."

"Incredible!" Yama exclaimed. "I've never heard of magic like that. We have to look into this some more. But first, we need to go find that scaredy dog."

CHAPTER

EIGHT

They found Wilder curled up against a tree. After helping him to his feet, Zeg gave him a long, strong hug, and the group headed back towards the village. When they arrived, they were greeted as heroes. Xand, Zeg and Yama thanked the villagers for their gratitude, while Wilder quietly slinked away from the crowd, ashamed of what he had done.

"Well, here are the heroes of Naran," said an older man. He approached everyone and thanked each of them personally. When he reached Wilder, he simply gave him a soft slap on the right side of the face. "We can talk about what happened later, all right?" he said.

"Sure," said Wilder quickly, having pulled up his cowl from his cloak to cover his head completely.

"I am Sheriff Terrubius. I cannot express how grateful I am for what you have done to protect this village," said Sheriff Terrubius. "I understand that you are looking to put a stop to the Gargoyle King. How interesting. Many have tried, and so far, none have succeeded. But I have a good feeling about you all!"

"We will put a stop to the Gargoyle King, rest assured!" said Zeg, his voice loud as always, but his tone much less confident than his usual boastful self.

"Here, you may need this," Terrubius said, pulling out an old and tattered parchment and unrolling it. "This map has information about an old Centaur, Mythranos, who legend has it knows the location of a weapon you can use to defeat the Gargoyle King.

He lives in the Fungus Forest, the second island of our realm," said Sheriff Terrubius, pointing at an area of the map with four islands. "Enter his kingdom with peace, or he may send his troops. Or his general might. Mythranos is very forgiving, but his general is quite concerned with the protection of his forest."

"Thank you. We will be sure to meet with…," said Xand, being unable to pronounce the name correctly.

"High Centaur Mythranos. I know him," said Yama. "Unfortunately," she added quietly to herself, but loud enough for Xand to hear. She realized that mentioning this might not have been the brightest idea, but the Sheriff simply smiled at her.

"It is the least I can do for all the help you have given us. I am glad someone has met Mythranos before. Make sure to tell him I send my regards and that I miss our talks," said Sheriff Terrubius.

The villagers invited them to have some of the stew from Madam Lauren, and gave them some supplies they would need for their coming adventure.

"Good luck," Terrubius called after them. "We will all need it!"

EPILOGUE

T he next morning, after some rest, Xand awoke with a start. He had been having another odd dream. He was in the city with metal castles again, but this time he was soaring above it on what looked like an orange hawk. He couldn't remember any other details when he was awake, except the hawk turning to him and saying, "Hold on!"

Xand looked to where Zeg had fallen asleep, but Zeg wasn't there. Xand went around the village and spotted his friend in the market going from booth to booth. He caught up to him and said, "Zeg, what are you looking for?"

"Nothing really. I bought this, though," he said, holding up a shiny golden key shaped like a dragon with red stones for eyes. Xand stared at it – and thought for a second the eyes were glowing. He looked up at Zeg to see if he saw it too, but when he looked back at the eyes, they were the same dull red stone with specks of dirt on them as when Zeg had first held it up.

"Why did you buy that?" Xand asked.

Zeg replied, "Looked cool."

"Did you buy what it opens?" Xand asked.

"Nope!" Zeg exclaimed.

Xand sighed. "Okay, well, let's get moving."

The friends circled back to find Yama and Wilder and prepared to set out for the Fungus Forest.

THE END

MANAM PUBLISHING